Bake a Wish

The Cheer-Up Cupcakes

Bake a Wish

The Cheer-Up Cupcakes

Lorna Honeywell

Illustrated by Samantha Chaffey

SCHOLASTIC INC.

ISBN 978-0-545-55236-3

Text copyright © 2012 by Hothouse Fiction Limited
Illustrations copyright © 2012 by Samantha Chaffey

12 11 10 9 8 7 6 5 4 3 2 1   13 14 15 16 17 18/0

Printed in the U.S.A.   40
First Scholastic printing, January 2013

*For my mother, Kitty Morrison, also
affectionately known as Granny Orkney.*

*And for Auriol Bussell,
the best grandma anyone could wish for.*

A Bad Case of the Grumps

Lily Dalton rushed out of her classroom as fast as she could. She had gotten a gold star on her English homework and she couldn't wait to tell Grandma!

As she ran onto the playground, she looked around for the bright-red coat that Grandma always wore. Lily grinned as she spotted her waiting with Lily's little brother, Archie, by the willow tree.

Today Grandma was looking extra colorful because she was wearing her red coat *and* her blue shoes, and she had a flowered scarf wrapped around her shoulders.

Grandma waved as she saw Lily, but Archie didn't. Archie was only four, and his daycare always ended earlier than Lily's elementary school. But both of them finished before Mom and Dad got home from work, so they always went back to Grandma's house after school. They stayed with her and Grandpa until Mom or Dad came to pick them up.

Archie looked just like Lily. They had the same wavy brown hair, although Lily's was long and Archie's was short. They both had chocolate-brown eyes and dimples in their cheeks when they smiled.

But Archie wasn't smiling now. In fact, he didn't look very happy at all, Lily thought as she hurried over to them.

"Hi, Grandma!" She grinned and reached up for a hug. "Hi, Archie!" Lily tried to hug him, too, but Archie just crossed his arms sulkily.

"How was school today, Lilybee?" Grandma asked.

Lily's smile grew even wider. "Miss Peters gave me a gold star!"

Grandma was so pleased that she gave Lily another hug. "Oh, good job!"

"Can I have a lucky dip?" Lily asked. "Please!"

Grandma pretended to think about it for a minute. "Ooh, yes, I think so."

Lily dipped her hand in Grandma's coat pocket. There was always some kind of tasty treat in there. You never knew what you would find! Lily pulled out a toffee in a shiny wrapper.

"Do you want a candy, Archie?"
Grandma asked, but he just scowled
and turned his head away. "Oh, dear."
Grandma made a worried face at Lily
over Archie's head. "I don't think you've
had a very good day, have you?"

Archie shook his head and stuck his
bottom lip out in a pout.

"Come on," Grandma said as she took
his hand. "Let's go home."

Grandpa was digging in the vegetable
patch when they walked through the
backyard. He pushed his hat back from
his face and smiled. "Hello, Lily. Hello,
Archie. How was school today?"

Lily rushed over and told him about
her gold star. Grandpa picked her up and
swung her around.

"We have a genius in the family!" he

joked as she squealed happily. Then he saw Archie's grumpy face. "Why don't you put your rain boots on and come help in the garden, Archie? I just saw a worm in the cabbage patch." Grandpa stretched his arms wide. "It was thi-i-s big."

Lily knew Archie loved being in the garden with Grandpa, especially if there were really big worms around. But Archie just shook his head and marched into the house.

"Oh, dear," Grandpa said. "Somebody's not in a very good mood."

"I know," Lily whispered. "He's been like this all the way home."

"Well, I hope he cheers up soon," Grandpa said as he went back to his digging.

Lily followed Archie and Grandma into the kitchen. She watched as Archie pulled off his shoes and dropped his bag on the floor. He walked right past Grandma's ginger-striped cat, Hector, who was lying on the kitchen windowsill, enjoying the warm sunshine pouring in through the window.

Hector jumped down when he saw Archie. He purred loudly, ready for the tummy rub Archie usually gave him, but

Archie didn't even look at him. Now Lily knew there was something *seriously* wrong.

Grandma sat down and pulled Archie up onto her lap. Lily sat on the floor at their feet and began to pet Hector.

"Now, then," Grandma said to Archie. "Why don't you tell me what's wrong and let's see if we can make it better."

Archie's bottom lip wobbled, and his voice was so quiet that Grandma and Lily had to lean in close to hear him. "I lost my pen." He sniffed and looked at Lily with big tears in his eyes. "My dinosaur pen."

"I'm sure it's around somewhere," Lily said, comforting him.

But Archie wasn't finished yet. "And Miss Dawn wasn't at school so we had to do extra *counting*. I can't do counting! I *hate* numbers."

"Oh, dear," said Grandma. "You *have* had a bad day." She stroked his hair gently. "Miss Dawn will probably be back tomorrow and we can ask Mommy and Daddy about the pen. So let's cheer up. What would you like to do this afternoon?"

"Nothing," Archie declared. "I'm too sad."

Lily sighed. She hated seeing her little brother so gloomy. "Isn't there anything we can do to cheer him up, Grandma?" she asked. "Something really special?"

Grandma looked like she was thinking very hard. "Hmmm . . ." She glanced at Lily and then at Archie. His bottom lip was sticking out as far as it could go. "This is the *worst* case of the grumps I've ever seen!" Grandma declared. "Something has to be done." She turned to the old cat lying stretched out on the floor. "Do you think it's time, Hector?"

Hector raised his head and purred.

Lily was curious and a little excited, too. She wound her hair around and around her finger. "Time for what, Grandma?"

Grandma clapped her hands and smiled. "Hector and I know just the thing to cheer Archie up!" Archie scrambled off her lap as she stood up and walked over to the large cabinet where she kept her best plates and china teapots.

Lily and Archie watched as Grandma stood on her tiptoes to reach the top shelf. Hector was watching her, too. He meowed softly as Grandma lifted down a large white jar decorated with yellow stripes.

As Grandma gently put the jar on the table, the kitchen felt very still for a moment. Then Hector leaped onto a chair at the table. At the same time, a sudden breeze blew in through the open window, making Lily's skirt flutter, and the old cuckoo clock on the wall began to sound.

"Cuckoo! Cuckoo!" the wooden bird sang four times before disappearing back inside the clock.

"What's happening?" Archie asked.

Grandma smiled and tapped the jar. "I'm going to show you something very special."

Archie went over to the table and Lily helped him climb up into his seat. "A jar?" Archie frowned.

"Ah, but not an *ordinary* jar," Grandma told him.

Lily's stomach hopped with excitement. "Is there something good inside it?"

Grandma smiled slyly and nodded. *"Magic,"* she whispered.

Lily's eyes opened as wide as they could go. "Magic?"

Archie was suddenly a lot more interested. He sat up in his chair and stared at the jar. "What's magic about it?"

Grandma put her hand on the lid. "First we need to make a wish." She smiled. "What should we wish for?"

"An elephant?" Archie suggested.

"We could do that, but I don't think it would fit in the kitchen." Grandma chuckled. "What about something that we really need?"

"I know!" Lily exclaimed. "Let's wish that Archie's bad mood goes away!"

"Yes," Archie grumbled. "I don't like being upset."

"Good idea, Lily!" Grandma smiled.

Lily closed her eyes and put her hands on the cool pottery. The jar felt smooth under her fingers. "I wish that Archie's bad mood goes away," she whispered.

"I wish my bad mood goes away," Archie mumbled. "And that I could do my counting," he added quickly.

"Can we look inside?" Lily asked, jumping up and down with excitement.

"Are you sure you're ready to open it?" Grandma teased.

"Yes!" Archie and Lily shouted together.

Sunlight glinted off a vase on the windowsill, filling the kitchen with rainbows. Lily and Archie gasped with excitement as she carefully opened the jar. As she pulled off the lid, she smiled. "Let the magic begin."

Grandma's Yummy Cupboard

Lily and Archie squeezed close together and stared at the open jar. Lily wondered what the magic might do. She loved reading books about fairies, but she never thought that there would be real, live magic in Grandma's kitchen!

"Look inside." Grandma smiled. Archie leaned back a bit nervously. Lily peered into the jar.

"What can you see?" he asked.

"Chocolate chips!" Lily exclaimed. "And

some little muffin cups. Oh! And a piece of rolled-up paper."

Grandma put her hand into the jar and took out the paper. "Would you read it for us, Lily?"

Lily uncurled the paper carefully.

Archie moved a little closer. "Is it a spell?" he asked. "In my cartoon a wizard said a spell that went KA-BOOM!"

Lily shook her head as she looked at it.

There was a list of ingredients and directions for cooking. "It's a recipe!" she cried. "But it doesn't say what it makes," she said, passing it to Grandma.

"Aha!" Grandma read the recipe and her eyes twinkled. "Well, isn't that lucky?

This is a recipe for Cheer-Up Cupcakes! Anyone who eats them will instantly be in a good mood."

Lily gasped. "But how did it get into the jar?"

Grandma shrugged her shoulders. "Magic!" She grinned. "This jar always gives me just the recipe I need to make a wish come true."

"So it'll fix Archie's bad mood?" Lily asked.

"Most definitely," Grandma said, nodding her head firmly.

"Oh, good!" Lily smiled. "You hear that, Archie? You can eat one and then you won't be in a bad mood anymore!"

Archie smiled at that. He got up on his knees in his chair and looked into the jar. "But where are the cupcakes?" he moaned.

"We're going to follow the recipe and

bake them," Grandma told him. "A recipe is like a spell, Archie. It turns lots of different ingredients into something extra delicious. But you have to help make the magic happen."

"That'll take forever!" Archie complained.

"Come on, Archie, it'll be fun," Lily said. "We're making a real magic potion!" Lily wiggled her fingers and cackled like a witch, but Archie didn't even smile.

Grandma took the muffin cups and chocolate chips out of the jar and rolled up her sleeves. "Lily, why don't you go and get aprons for you and Archie to wear?"

Lily rushed to where Grandma's aprons were hanging on a hook behind the kitchen door. She'd eaten plenty of delicious cakes and biscuits that Grandma had baked, but she'd never helped her make them . . . and now she was baking something *magical*! If they started making the cupcakes now, then they should be ready before Mom and Dad picked them up.

While Lily put on a pretty apron covered with big red flowers, Grandma helped Archie into a blue-and-white-striped one and tied it for him. It was much too big, and Archie looked funny with the apron trailing down to his toes. Lily giggled. Archie pouted.

"Maybe I'll have to find you some aprons of your own for next time," Grandma said.

"One with dinosaurs on it?" Archie asked hopefully.

"Perhaps." Grandma turned on the oven. "Now, whenever we do any cooking, the first thing we have to do is wash our

hands. The second thing we do is put some music on!" She laughed, turning a knob on the radio so that the kitchen was filled with the happy music Grandma always listened to.

Lily and Archie rushed over to the kitchen sink. Once their hands were clean, Grandma showed them where she kept her baking ingredients. It was a large cupboard, big enough for Lily and Archie to stand inside.

Lily looked up in wonder. Every shelf was full of jars and bottles, bags and packets. Lily could see cake decorations, birthday candles, marzipan, and icing. Best of all, the cupboard smelled amazing!

Her nose twitched as she breathed in the sweet scent. "I can smell toasted marshmallows!" she said.

Archie licked his lips. "I can smell popcorn . . . and jelly and . . . um . . . chocolate."

"I'm going to call this the Yummy Cupboard." Lily smiled.

Grandma laughed. "Why don't I read the recipe out loud and you two can bring the ingredients over to the table?"

Lily was so excited she started bouncing on the spot. She and Archie were so lucky. They had the best grandma in the world. She was as cuddly as a koala bear, was never, ever grumpy, *and* she had a magic baking jar!

Grandma began reading from the recipe. "First, we need self-rising flour. That's what makes the cakes grow when you bake them. It's in a blue-and-white paper bag."

"I'll get it!" Archie said. But the flour was too high for him to reach. He jumped up and down and stretched his arms out, but it was no good. "Darn," he grumped.

Lily giggled. She could reach the shelf

easily. "Here you go," she said as she passed it down to him. Archie held it

so tightly that a small white cloud of flour puffed up from the bag and settled on his head, turning his hair white. He looked as old as Grandpa! Lily laughed again, but Archie scowled.

Uh-oh, Lily thought, *Archie's bad mood isn't over yet!* Luckily, Grandma ruffled his hair to brush the flour away, and kissed him on the top of his head. Then, before he could get upset, she read out the next ingredient.

"This is fun," Lily said. "It's just like a treasure hunt!"

Working together, Lily and Archie found cocoa powder, sugar, and butter, and put them all next to the magic jar.

Grandma read out the next ingredient. "Now we need vanilla extract. It's in a tiny bottle. It looks like something a fairy might use!" Lily and Archie raced past each other, rushing to get to the cupboard. Suddenly, Lily spotted some teeny bottles, half hidden behind a jar of molasses.

"Got it! Vanilla extract!" she cried.

"Good job, Lily." Grandma smiled. "And well done, Archie, too," she added quickly, as his face crumpled.

Grandma had already put a large mixing bowl on the table next to the measuring cups, with some spoons, a whisk, and a sieve.

"What next, Grandma?" Archie asked.

"Now"—Grandma clapped her hands—
"we're ready to begin!"

An Eggy Adventure

"Silly me!" said Grandma as she stared
at the baking ingredients laid out on
the table. "I almost forgot the eggs." She
turned to Archie and Lily. "Lilybee, would
you take Archie out to the chicken coop
and see if Jessie and Bessie have laid any
today?"

Lily started pulling her rain boots on.
She loved Grandma's chickens, and she
usually fed them their corn before she
went home each evening.

But Archie wasn't
putting his boots
on. "We can't
go outside," he
moaned. "It's
raining."

Lily looked
out the window.
Raindrops were
trickling down
the windowpane.
Grandma looked
up at a small gray
cloud covering
the sun. "It's just
a little shower. It'll be over in a minute."

"But I'll get wet," Archie insisted.

"Well, you're not made of sugar,"
Grandma told him. "You won't melt!"

"Come on, Archie." Lily opened the

back door. "We can pretend we're in a *rain* forest. There might be wild animals out there." Lily made her eyes wide and frightened. "Monkeys and lizards and tigers."

"OK!" Archie rushed to the door and quickly put on his raincoat and boots. Then he dashed outside. "I'm ready first," he told Lily. "That makes me the leader."

Lily didn't mind. At least he wasn't being so grumpy. Grandma stood at the door watching them as they set off toward the chicken coop. "Remember to ask Jessie and Bessie nicely for the eggs," she called after them. "And make sure you say thank you."

They set off down the narrow garden path between the vegetable patch and the strawberry plants, all the time looking out for pretend crocodiles and snakes.

The rain drizzled down, coating the garden in sparkling drops. Archie picked up a long twig and held it like a sword. When they came to the tall rhubarb stalks, he pushed the large leaves aside.

"What can you see?" Lily whispered as Hector stalked past her and rubbed his head against her leg.

"Tiger!" Archie shouted. "Run!"

Hector gave a surprised *meow* and rushed back to the safety of the kitchen as Lily and Archie ran shrieking and laughing to the chicken coop.

The coop had a triangular shed where Jessie and Bessie slept, and a run covered with wire mesh where they could walk around and scratch at the ground. It was just big enough for Grandma to go in if she bent over, and Lily and Archie fit inside easily.

Lily opened the door and dashed into the run. Archie left his stick outside and followed Lily. She made sure to close the door after them. They didn't want the chickens escaping or, worse still, tigers getting in.

It was very dark, but nice and warm, and it smelled of wood and straw. Bessie and Jessie were resting in their nests, sheltering from the rain.

"Hello, girls!" Lily said, just like Grandma always did. "Do you have any eggs for us?"

Bessie clucked softly and stood up. Beneath her was a warm brown egg.

But Jessie stayed snuggled

in her nest. She tilted her head to one side and blinked at Archie. Archie stared at her. "She's not getting up."

"Don't worry," Lily told him. "I know what to do." She reached up to a plastic tub on a shelf above the nests and pulled off the lid. "Let's give them some corn," she told Archie. She scattered a handful of the corn on the floor of the shed. Bessie flew down and started pecking at it, and moments later Jessie stood up and ruffled her feathers.

"Look!" Archie said. He was pointing to a white egg lying in her nest. He stood back as Jessie made a soft clucking sound and flapped down to the floor. While she pecked at the corn, Archie collected the eggs.

"That's one egg from Bessie and one from Jessie," Lily told him. She smiled at her little brother as he carefully picked the eggs up. "How many eggs does that make?"

Archie looked down at his hands. "Two!" he told her.

"Good job, Archie!" Lily cried. "See, you *can* do your counting!"

She put the tub of grain up on the shelf. "Let's get back to the kitchen. I want to start baking." Then she remembered something.

"Thank you for the eggs," she told the chickens. "We're going to make magical cupcakes with them!"

Bessie and Jessie clucked again. Lily leaned down to Archie. "Do you know what they said?" she asked. Archie shook his head, his brown eyes wide. "They said, *'Sounds delicious!'*"

Lily and Archie both laughed as they raced back through the garden. The rain had stopped and the sun was out again. Lily had forgotten all about crocodiles, snakes, and tigers. Instead she was imagining the taste of delicious cupcakes.

Lily reached the back door first. "Come on," she called to Archie, tugging off her boots before hurrying inside. Archie rushed up to the doorway holding the eggs. He kicked off his right boot, but when he tried to wiggle his left foot free, Archie lost his balance and started to fall over.

"Oh . . . oh . . . *oh!*" he cried, and toppled to the ground with a bump.

Lily turned around just in time to see

Archie burst into tears. He was lying on his back, and there in his hand was a mess of yolk and shell where an egg used to be.

Mixing Up Some Magic

Grandma came running out into the yard. Lily was still staring at her little brother. In one hand, Archie was holding Bessie's brown egg, but the fingers of his other hand were covered in runny gloop and bits of white shell.

"Never mind," Grandma said cheerfully, "it doesn't matter."

Archie's cheeks were pink and his eyes were full of tears. When he spoke, his voice shook. "I broke an egg," he sobbed. "We can't make the cupcakes now."

"There, there, don't worry," Grandma said, passing the smooth brown egg to Lily.

Lily felt like she was about to cry, too, as she stared at the egg. She'd wanted to cook magical cupcakes so much, and now everything was ruined. The Cheer-Up Cupcakes had made Archie feel even *worse*!

"Come on, let's wash your hands, Archie," Grandma was saying. Inside, Archie cried even harder as Grandma washed the gloopy egg off his fingers.

"Hmmm, it looks like we need the Cheer-Up Cupcakes more than ever," Grandma said thoughtfully.

"But we can't make them now!" Archie wailed.

"Yes we can," Grandma said. "We just need to find another egg. There might still be one from yesterday in the fridge. Lily, why don't you go and look?"

Lily ran over to the fridge, her heart beating fast. Before she opened it, she closed her eyes for a second and wished as hard as she could. *Please let there be an egg inside.* She wanted to make the Cheer-Up Cupcakes so much. She tugged at the fridge door and peered in. There was lots of yummy-looking food, but there were no eggs.

Lily's heart sank. Archie was going to be sadder than ever now that they couldn't make Cheer-Up Cupcakes. She sighed and pushed the door closed. But as she did, something caught her eye. There, on the inside of the door, were two brown eggs!

"Grandma! Archie! Look!" Lily yelled as

she held them up. "Don't worry. There were two eggs in the fridge the whole time."

"Phew!" Grandma smiled with relief. "See," she said, giving Archie a hug. "It's OK after all. And we've even got one spare for my breakfast tomorrow. Now go and wash your hands again and then we can start making some cake!" Archie sniffed and gave a watery smile, then went off to the bathroom.

"While Archie's doing that, I've got a job for you, Lily," Grandma said. "It's called 'creaming' the butter and sugar, but it just means mixing them together."

Lily plopped the soft butter into a bowl while Grandma measured out the right amount of sugar. Then Lily tipped the sugar on top of the butter and started pushing the crunchy crystals into the butter with a fork.

"That's it!" Grandma smiled. "Keep going until it goes white and creamy."

Lily mixed until her arm hurt. "Is it done yet?" she asked Grandma, peering anxiously into the bowl.

"Let's have a look." Grandma whisked the fork through the mixture much more quickly than Lily had done, and soon it started to look creamy and delicious. Lily licked her lips excitedly!

Archie rushed back in and peered into the bowl excitedly. "What can I do?" he asked as Grandma tied his apron back on.

"Do you want to break the eggs, Archie?" Grandma asked. "In the bowl this time!" Grandma rolled up his sleeves and showed him how to tap the egg against the edge of the bowl until the shell cracked. With Grandma and Lily's help, Archie broke both the eggs into the bowl without getting any shell in it.

"Next we add the vanilla extract," Grandma said. "The vanilla makes the cupcakes extra tasty. Do you want to smell it?"

She opened the bottle and Archie and Lily scrambled over to sniff it. Archie put his nose to the open bottle and breathed in deeply. "Mmmm!" he cried. "It smells like ice cream."

"Can I put it in?"
Lily asked. The top
of the tiny fairy-
sized bottle was
a little dropper,
and Lily really
wanted to play
with it.

Grandma gave her the bottle and Lily
carefully squeezed the top so that a few
drops fell into the bowl.

"Now I have a *very* important job for
you, Archie," Grandma said when he'd
finished sniffing the vanilla bottle. She
handed Archie the sieve. "I need you to
sift the flour."

The sieve was made of silver metal with
lots of tiny little holes in it. "It looks like
a fishing net," Archie said. He held it still

while Grandma poured the flour into
it. She showed him how to gently shake
it from side to side so the flour drifted
through.

Then Archie frowned. "Why does it
have to go through it?"

"To get rid of all the lumps," Grandma

told him. "You don't want to bite into a lovely chocolatey cupcake and find a big lump of flour in it, do you?"

Mmmmm. Lily licked her lips. The thought of a tasty cupcake was already making her stomach rumble!

Grump in the Garden

"Can I stir? Can I stir?" Archie jumped up and down.

"Yes," Grandma told him. "We just need to add the cocoa powder to make it chocolatey! Can you measure out two tablespoons?"

Archie peered suspiciously at the brown powder. "It doesn't look like chocolate," he said as he dipped the measuring spoon in. Lily agreed. She was glad they were putting real chocolate chips in, too!

"Just you wait until it's all mixed in with the other ingredients," Grandma said. "Why don't you hold the bowl still, Lily, and we'll take turns stirring."

Once the cocoa powder was added, Lily put her hands on either side of the bowl as Archie's spoon went around and around and all the ingredients turned into a thick chocolatey goo. She could hardly believe that eggs and flour and cocoa powder turned into something that looked so delicious. It was magical!

"Can we put the chocolate chips in now?" Archie asked excitedly.

Grandma's eyes twinkled. "I think we should treat ourselves to two chips each first, don't you?" she said, opening the package. "Would you like to count them out, Archie?"

"I'll help!" Lily offered, but Grandma stopped her.

"Let's see if Archie can do it by himself."

Lily felt angry for a second, but Grandma put her finger to her lips and smiled. Lily realized that Grandma was trying to get Archie to practice his counting. She watched her little brother as he leaned over the chocolate chips.

Archie pushed two chocolate chips toward Grandma and put two in Lily's palm. He counted them out on his fingers. "One . . . two . . . three . . . four." He popped another two into his mouth. "Five . . . six!" he said, giving them a big chocolatey grin.

"Good job!" Lily praised him. Grandma gave him a hug.

"Do I get a prize?" Archie asked.

"Yes, you can have a cupcake—
when they're done!" Grandma joked.
Archie looked longingly at the rest of
the chocolate chips, but he emptied
the bag into the bowl and continued
stirring.

Lily picked up the recipe from the table and began reading it. "Almost finished," she said. "What's next, Grandma?" she asked.

Grandma had her head in a cupboard. "Here it is!" she cried, putting a tin on the table. It had lots of holes in it, just the right size to fit the muffin cups in. "Can you put a muffin cup in each of the holes, Lilybee?" Grandma asked.

Lily popped open the box and took out the pretty paper cups. They were a light blue color and they were covered with tiny pink polka dots.

"Make sure you only put one cup in each," Grandma told her. "Sometimes they stick together." Lily licked her fingers and rubbed the sides of the muffin cups to separate them.

Grandma let Lily spoon the mixture carefully into the cups. Archie helped by telling her which ones needed a little more in them. Then they both scraped the bowl clean, making sure they got every last bit out. Afterward, Grandma let them lick their wooden spoons.

"Mmmmm," Lily said between licks. "I think our Cheer-Up Cupcakes are going to be the best ever."

Archie agreed. "The best in the whole wide world!"

"*Meow!*" Hector added. He was sitting at Lily's feet, looking up at her hungrily.

"Sorry, Hector, you can't have any," Lily told him. "Chocolate isn't good for cats." Hector gave a small, disappointed *meow* and looked at Archie, but he was busy licking his chocolatey fingers.

"I'm sure we can find a treat for you, too, Hector," Grandma laughed. "We just need to get this in the oven first. The cupcakes need to bake for twenty minutes."

"Twenty minutes?" Archie wailed. "That's a long time!"

Grandma put the pan in the oven and shut the door. "Why don't you go into the yard and play until they're done?"

Lily stared at the oven. She wanted to stay and watch—she'd never seen magical cupcakes cooking before. Maybe there would be sparkles and fireworks in the oven as the magic baked!

Archie was looking longingly at the oven, too. A delicious sweet smell was already starting to come from it.

"The cupcakes won't bake any faster

if you watch them," Grandma told them. "I'll let you know when they're ready."

Archie gave a grumpy moan as he took his apron off and plodded over to where his boots were lying at the back door. "I want them to be ready NOW!" he grumbled.

"Come on, Archie," Lily said, reluctantly going outside. "We can go and see if Grandpa's found any more worms."

It was bright and sunny now that the rain shower had passed. She could see Grandpa down at the far end of the garden. His hat was bobbing up and down as he dug in the vegetable patch. Hector was busily lapping up fresh rainwater from a small puddle.

Archie sat down on the garden bench and folded his arms. "I'm still not happy," he pouted.

"That's because you haven't eaten the

cupcakes yet." Lily told him. She picked up a bright-red ball lying behind a flowerpot. "Let's play catch."

She threw the ball in a high arc. Archie reached his hands up, but the ball bounced down on his head.

"OW!" Archie cried.

"Oops! Sorry!" Lily called, but she couldn't help giggling. Archie kicked the ball grumpily and it flew up, higher and higher—right over the fence!

Lily's stomach jumped with worry. Suddenly, there was an angry shout from the yard next-door. "Hey! Who did that?" someone yelled. Then they heard the heavy thump of feet stomping across the ground toward them.

"Uh-oh," Lily whispered. "I think we're in trouble."

Baking Magic

Lily and Archie stared in horror as a face peered over the top of the fence. It was Grandma's neighbor Mr. Mellor, and he looked very angry. His gray mustache was twitching and his eyes had almost disappeared beneath his thick eyebrows.

"Who threw that ball into my garden?" He frowned down at them. "You should be more careful. It landed on my tulips."

Lily felt her cheeks turn pink. "Sorry, Mr. Mellor." She took a deep breath. "We didn't mean to. Please can we have our ball back?"

"No, you can't," he growled. "That way it won't land in my garden again." He disappeared behind the fence still muttering, "Careless children . . . squashing my tulips."

Archie looked as if he was going to cry. Lily squeezed her little brother's hand, but she was upset, too. It felt terrible to be yelled at. Archie hadn't kicked the ball over the fence on purpose, and she hadn't meant to hit him in the head. Mr. Mellor was a big meanie and now he'd made her feel grumpy, too. It wasn't fair!

Lily was feeling so upset that she almost said something mean when Archie started sniffing. But suddenly she smelled it, too. She sniffed the air again and again. There was a delicious smell drifting through the open window!

"The cupcakes!" Archie whispered.

Lily and Archie rushed to the back door. Lily helped Archie take his boots off this time. Lily could hear Grandma inside, singing along to the radio. They had just made it into the kitchen when the timer went *ding*. Lily looked at Archie with delight and hurried inside. Grandma was already lifting the hot tray out of the oven with her oven mitts.

"Are they ready?" Lily asked.

"Almost," Grandma said, setting the hot tin down. "They'll have to cool down before we can eat them. We should start making the icing." She turned around and saw Lily's and Archie's miserable faces.

"What's wrong now?" she asked.

"Our ball went into Mr. Mellor's yard," Lily told her, "and he yelled at us, even though it was an accident."

"And he won't give it back!" Archie started to cry and untied his apron.

Grandma bent down and wiped the tears from his eyes. "Oh, dear. I think we need a little cheer-up magic right now, don't you?"

Archie sniffed and nodded his head as hard as he could.

Grandma carefully picked up one of the cupcakes. "They're still too hot to eat," she said, but she unwrapped a small one and broke it in half. She gently blew on the pieces before handing them to Archie and Lily. "But I think you can try these bits."

Lily put the piece of cake in her mouth. Seconds later, warm, soft, fluffy, chocolatey cake spread out on her tongue.

It was so delicious, she closed her eyes and gave a long happy sigh. "This is *magically* good!" she whispered.

Archie had stopped sniffing. As he bit into his piece of cupcake his brown eyes grew wide, and his smile grew even wider. Soon he was nibbling it happily.

"Better?" Grandma asked, with a twinkle in her eye.

Archie nodded his head up and down. Just then, the microwave *ping*ed.

"That's the icing," Grandma said, putting two bowls of melted chocolate on the table, along with a bowl of chocolate

buttons and some glittery sprinkles from
her favorite baking-supply store, the
Tasty Cupboard. Lily grinned, and
Archie licked his
lips in glee. Their
Cheer-Up Cupcakes
were going to be
beautiful!

"If we each
decorate half the
cupcakes, how
many will we have,
Archie?" Lily asked

as she spooned the runny chocolate
over one of her cakes, then took a
pinch of sprinkles and scattered them
on top.

"Six!" Archie grinned as Grandma
retied his apron on for him.

"Good job!" Lily smiled as she looked

at her cupcake. It looked so pretty—
almost too nice to eat! Archie was
dipping the cakes right into the
chocolate and giggling as he dribbled
chocolate all over the table and all
over himself. "It's a good thing you're
wearing an apron!" Grandma said as

she went to get
them all a drink.

When she was
sure Grandma
wasn't looking,
Lily dipped
the tip of her
finger into the
smooth melted
chocolate. It tasted just as good as she
had expected. Thick and chocolatey
and sweet! She glanced back over her
shoulder. Grandma was busy helping

Archie spoon chocolate on one of his cakes. Lily dipped her finger into the chocolate again. "Mmmm," she said, and closed her eyes.

"Lily?" Grandma's voice made her jump. "Have you been eating the melted chocolate?"

Lily opened her eyes. Grandma's hands were on her hips, but she didn't look mad.

Lily gasped. "How did you know?"

Grandma winked. "Magic," she said. "And because you're all messy. You've got chocolate all around your mouth!"

By the time Grandma had poured them each a glass of milk and made herself a pot of tea in the old brown teapot, Archie had decorated all of his cupcakes. Lily was just starting her third one, carefully arranging chocolate buttons on the top so they made the shape of a flower. "Please can we eat one now, Grandma?" Archie begged.

"Okay, go ahead," Grandma said. Archie grinned and took an enormous bite of one of his cupcakes. Lily couldn't resist, either, and unpeeled the wrapper on one of hers. The chocolate was still wet and gooey and made a mess all over her fingers, but she didn't care! She bit into the cake and felt happiness spread through her. Cheer-Up Cupcakes were delicious!

Just then, Grandpa came in from the garden carrying a tub of freshly picked lettuce. "Mmmm, something smells tasty," he said.

"We made Cheer-Up Cupcakes," Lily told him. "They're magic!"

"Oh, really?" Grandpa asked. He washed his hands and sat down in his usual place at the kitchen table. "What's magical about Cheer-Up Cupcakes?" he asked.

"Anyone who eats them is instantly in a good mood!" Lily explained. "And they work! Archie's bad mood has completely disappeared!"

Archie nodded happily. His mouth was too full of cake to speak.

"In that case, I can't wait to taste them," Grandpa said. "I'm in *such* a bad mood," he joked, making a horrible grumpy face. Lily and Archie laughed. "Which one can I have?" Grandpa asked. "They all look so delicious!"

"This one!" Archie cried, giving one to Grandpa. "It's got the most chocolate buttons."

Lily watched as he took a bite and slowly chewed it. A smile spread across Grandpa's face.

"Well, Grandma's baking is always good," he said, jumping up to give Grandma a kiss on her cheek. "But this is the best cupcake

I have ever tasted." He looked at his feet. "I think I can feel the magic."

"Can you?" Lily asked. "Really?"

Grandpa nodded. "Yes, my toes are tingling and I can't stop smiling."

"I can't, either!" Lily laughed.

"Me, neefer!" Archie said with his mouth full of cake. Lily grinned as she looked around at everyone's happy faces. The Cheer-Up Cupcakes had worked their magic, just like Grandma said they would.

Lily's Idea

Once everyone had eaten a cupcake, they sat back happily. Hector purred loudly as he lapped at a saucer of milk, and Archie slurped from his own glass so fast that he got a milk mustache.

"That was so much fun," Lily told Grandma once all the cakes were decorated. "I love baking magical cakes, and I love eating them even more!" Lily looked at the recipe lying on the table. It was dotted with spots and splashes of cake mixture now. "Can we keep the recipe, Grandma?"

"Of course," Grandma said. "You never know when we might need to make Cheer-Up Cupcakes again. I've got just the place for you to keep it."

Grandma went into her Yummy Cupboard to search the shelves for something. "Here it is." She carried a box covered in a lovely flower pattern over to the table and set it down next to Lily. "You can put all your magical recipes in here."

Lily gave Grandma a big thank-you hug. "Now we can make Cheer-Up Cupcakes whenever we want to!" She put the recipe in the box and Grandma put it up on the shelf next to the jar.

Lily sat down at the table and looked up at the jar happily. Archie was making happy *brrrrrrum*ing noises beside her as he ran his toy truck over the tabletop. Grandpa sat in his chair, reading the newspaper.

"I wonder what magical recipe will be in the jar next time?" Lily thought out loud. She couldn't imagine anything tasting better than Cheer-Up Cupcakes.

"Who knows?" Grandma smiled and shrugged her shoulders. "But I'm sure the magic will know *just* the right recipe to give us."

Lily looked thoughtful. "So whenever we need something, the jar will have a recipe for us?"

"Yes! That's because it's magical, silly!" Archie told her.

Lily gave her little brother a hug. It was so nice that he was back to his usual cheerful self. She wished everyone could be happy all the time.

Lily suddenly had an idea. Archie wasn't the only one who had been in a bad mood today. . . . She turned to Grandma excitedly. "Do you think the magic would work on Mr. Mellor?" she asked.

"I would think so," Grandma replied, a smile spreading over her face.

"We should take him a Cheer-Up Cupcake!" Lily cried.

"That's a very nice idea, Lilybee," Grandma said.

Lily didn't really want to visit scary Mr. Mellor, but she did want to see if the magic would work on him. She chose the prettiest cake with the most sprinkles, and Grandma put it on a plate for her. Lily took a deep breath and held Archie's hand. "Come on, Archie," she said, sounding braver than she felt.

Archie hid behind Lily as they walked next door and rang the doorbell. It wasn't a nice musical bell like Grandma's, but a buzzer that sounded like a very loud wasp.

The door opened and Mr. Mellor stared
down at them.

"What do you want?" he snapped.

"We're sorry our ball went in your
yard," Lily explained. Archie peered out
from behind her and nodded. Lily was

feeling less brave now that Mr. Mellor was glaring at her.

"It wasn't really Archie's fault," Lily explained. "It was the bad mood."

Archie nodded in agreement.

Mr. Mellor was still scowling. "Bad mood?" he asked.

"Yes," Lily told him. "Anyway, we brought you this," she said, holding the cupcake out in front of her. "We made them with Grandma this afternoon. It's a Cheer-Up Cupcake."

"Hmmm," Mr. Mellor said, taking the cupcake.

He didn't even say "thank you"! Lily thought to herself.

She and Archie watched as Mr. Mellor bit into the cake. He chewed so fast his mustache bounced up and down. But then his eyebrows lifted and his eyes opened wide. "Mmmmm!" he said.

He took another bite, and then another. Lily watched him closely to see if she could see the magic working.

"Isn't it yummy?" Archie said excitedly, as Mr. Mellor popped the last piece of cake into his mouth.

"Delicious," Mr. Mellor mumbled. "Er . . . thank you."

His mustache twitched and Lily saw a small smile curling the corners of his mouth. *It must be the magic!* Lily squeezed Archie's hand. Mr. Mellor wiped the crumbs from his mustache with the napkin and stared at them. "I suppose you want your ball back?"

Lily nodded. "Yes, please."

Mr. Mellor disappeared inside the house and Lily and Archie looked at each other. "It worked!" they said together.

Mr. Mellor came back and handed the ball to Archie. "Make sure you keep it away from my tulips," he warned.

Mr. Mellor still wasn't in a good mood, Lily decided. It would take a *lot* of cupcakes to do that, but at least he wasn't in *quite* such a bad mood.

Lily skipped all the way back down the path. Archie walked beside her, taking giant dinosaur strides. Archie counted his steps all the way back to Grandma's house and didn't make one mistake. "Lily!" he gasped. "I can do my counting, too!"

Lily squeezed his hand as he ran in to tell Grandma.

But the magic wasn't finished yet.

There was a surprise for Archie when they got back to Grandma's. Mom and Dad had arrived to take them home and were sitting at the kitchen table. "Look what I found in the car," Dad said. He held up Archie's lost dinosaur pen. "It must have fallen out of your backpack this morning."

Archie could hardly believe it. "I've had the best day ever!" he yelled.

"How was your day, Lily?" Mom asked.

Lily looked at the jar, back in its usual place on the shelf and sparkling brightly in a ray of sunshine. She felt her toes start to tingle and an extra big smile crossed her face.

"It was magical!"

RAINBOW magic™

There's Magic in Every Series!

The Rainbow Fairies
The Weather Fairies
The Jewel Fairies
The Pet Fairies
The Fun Day Fairies
The Petal Fairies
The Dance Fairies
The Music Fairies
The Sports Fairies
The Party Fairies
The Ocean Fairies
The Night Fairies
The Magical Animal Fairies
The Princess Fairies
The Superstar Fairies

Read them all!

scholastic.com
rainbowmagiconline.com

RMFAIRY7

RAINBOW magic™

SPECIAL EDITION

Three Books in Each One—
More Rainbow Magic Fun!

Joy the Summer Vacation Fairy

Holly the Christmas Fairy

Kylie the Carnival Fairy

Stella the Star Fairy

Shannon the Ocean Fairy

Trixie the Halloween Fairy

Gabriella the Snow Kingdom Fairy

Juliet the Valentine Fairy

Mia the Bridesmaid Fairy

Flora the Dress-Up Fairy

Paige the Christmas Play Fairy

Emma the Easter Fairy

Cara the Camp Fairy

Destiny the Rock Star Fairy

Belle the Birthday Fairy

Olympia the Games Fairy

Selena the Sleepover Fairy

Cheryl the Christmas Tree Fairy

Florence the Friendship Fairy

Lindsay the Luck Fairy

■SCHOLASTIC

scholastic.com
rainbowmagiconline.com

HIT entertai

RMSPEC

SOPHIE

Sophie knows she's special—now she just needs the perfect name to show it!

Sophie the AWESOME

by Lara Bergen

SCHOLASTIC

Sophie the HERO

by Lara Bergen

SCHOLASTIC

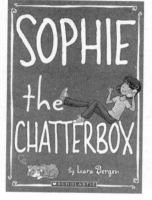

Sophie the CHATTERBOX

by Lara Bergen

SCHOLASTIC

Sophie the ZILLIONAIRE

by Lara Bergen

SCHOLASTIC

Sophie the SNOOP

by Lara Bergen

SCHOLASTIC

Sophie the DAREDEVIL

by Lara Bergen

SCHOLASTIC

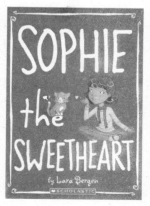

Sophie the SWEETHEART

by Lara Bergen

SCHOLASTIC

Lucky Stars ☆

It's a wish come true – read all of the books in the Lucky Stars series!

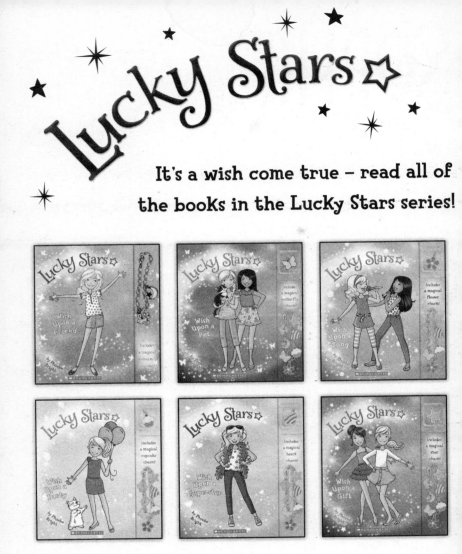

Each book comes with a magical charm!

You can make Cheer-Up Cupcakes, too!

WHAT YOU WILL NEED:

For the cupcakes:
¼ pound room-temperature unsalted butter
½ cup sugar
1 teaspoon vanilla extract
2 large eggs
1 cup self-rising flour
2 tablespoons cocoa powder
¾ cup chocolate chips
1–2 tablespoons milk

Makes 12 cupcakes

For the icing:
6 ounces milk chocolate
Sprinkles, chocolate buttons, or whatever cake decorations you have

Equipment:
Muffin tin
Muffin cups
Mixing bowl
1 small bowl
Sieve, fork, wooden spoons

THEN ASK A GROWN-UP TO HELP YOU:

1. Pre-heat the oven to 400 degrees.

2. Cream the butter and sugar together in a bowl with a fork.

3. Add the eggs and vanilla extract. Stir.

4. Sift the flour in and mix in the cocoa powder and chocolate chips.

5. Add one tablespoon of milk. If the mixture is too thick and stiff, then add one more tablespoon of milk.

6. Place the muffin cups in the muffin tin. Spoon the mixture into the muffin cups.

7. Bake in the oven for 12–15 minutes.

8. Heat the milk chocolate in the small bowl in the microwave until just melted.

9. Top the cupcakes with the chocolate and whatever cake decorations you have. Warning—this can get messy!

10. Share the Cheer-Up Cupcakes with someone in a bad mood to make them happy!

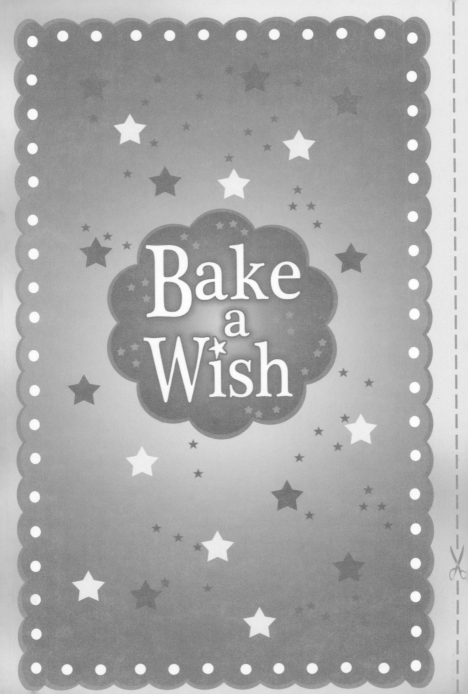